Heaven's Angel Food

WHEN YOU DESERVE THE VERY BEST

D1466801

de de Cox

CREDITS:

Female Model:	Heaven Redmon
Male Model:	Bo Cox
Dog Model:	Rocky (owners, Tiffany and Jacob Redmon)
Photography and Production:	Austin Ozier / Ozier Productions
HMUA:	Scooter Minyard
Asst. to HMUA:	Jeanette Moore
Wardrobe and Design:	Andre Wilson / Style Icon Group, LLC
Videography/Documentary:	Brooke Danielle Way
Location :	Redmon Family Home
Inspiration :	Elizabeth Cox (FURever in our memories)
Contributor:	Robyn Thomas

Quantity sales special discounts are available on quantity purchases by corporations, associations, and others. For details, contact the publisher at the address above.

Orders by U.S. trade bookstores and wholesalers. Email info@BeyondPublishing.net

The Beyond Publishing Speakers Bureau can bring authors to your live event. For more information or to book an event contact the Beyond Publishing Speakers Bureau speak@BeyondPublishing.net

The Author can be reached directly at BeyondPublishing.net

Manufactured and printed in the United States of America distributed globally by BeyondPublishing.net

BEYOND
PUBLISHING

New York | Los Angeles | London | Sydney

ISBN Softcover: 978-1-637922-00-2

Heaven's Angel Food

INTRO

In order to achieve her dreams, she would need to reveal what she had kept hidden for so long. She had never told anyone. There had never been a need. And now, her secret would be revealed in order to succeed with her passion and dreams. Whoever said the "truth will set you free" lied.

CHAPTER 1

Heaven shook her head to bring her back to the present and back to the task at hand – finishing the snacks for the children at the elementary school of Windermere, Connecticut. She was afraid that someone would find out. The only thing certain in Heaven's life was this moment. This was where she belonged.

She made her way to the entry of the Windermere Elementary School. She had individually wrapped 313 snack packs to distribute to the children for the weekend. Baking always took place from Tuesday through Thursday. Wrapping was Thursday evenings and then the drive to the chosen school for distribution to all students from K-5 took place on Fridays. All this preparation was done in Heaven's home. The time to make a decision to find a place that would expand Heaven's journey had come.

She parked her car in the visitor section of the school parking lot. She looked over in the passenger seat. Looking at Heaven with those deep, brown eyes was her companion and sidekick, Malcolm, who had been with Heaven since her arrival into the small town of Windermere, Kentucky. She recalled how she met her best friend. Her mind drifted back to the day she had arrived with nothing, but yet with everything.

Heaven stepped off the bus. She was free. She looked around to survey the small town of Windermere. The light flashing caught her eye. Not only did she see the hotel, but you could not miss the name – The New View Hotel. Heaven smiled. This town would now be her home. She had no clue what she was going to do when she walked through the entrance. She had a few dollars. As she drew close to the hotel, she heard a noise. It was coming from the side of the entrance of the hotel. She was a bit unsure if she should investigate or just walk in and do what she was there to do – get a room and rest. Instinct told her to keep walking. Curiosity told her to stop. She heard the noise again, except this time, it was a whimper. Something was in pain. Heaven could not just leave without looking further into what was behind that bush.

With caution, she pulled back the limbs of the bush and there, to her astonishment, was a dog. It was not small by any means. From the whining noise and the bearing of teeth, it was in full-blown attack mode. Heaven realized this was going to take extra effort on her part to even pull the dog forward so she could reach it. Where were gloves? Oh yeah, she only had the clothes on her back and a garbage bag, which contained nothing but all that she had accumulated in a short time. Isn't that what one escaped with when there was no turning back? All or nothing?

Heaven rummaged through the garbage bag. She reached inside to feel for a pair of socks. One pair. That was it. Well, they were being used for a good cause. She placed them on her hands and proceeded to approach the dog with caution. Using her voice as a distraction, her right hand had begun to rub the dog's paw in a circular motion. The teeth gnarling stopped, and the dog hunkered as close to the corner of the building as it could. Being cornered was no fun. Heaven knew from experience. Many times, she felt she had been placed in the corner and left to fend for herself. She did not want the dog to feel as if all hope was lost and be left alone to starve or die.

Throwing caution to the wind, she reached with her other hand covered with the sock and pulled the dog slowly towards her.

Heaven did not know if the dog was hurt or if it was just too tired to fight any longer. The dog no longer had its hairs raised off its back. The dog, with hesitation, came closer to Heaven. Heaven had no clue if it was a boy or a girl.

Heaven examined the dog as best she could. She needed to check in to the hotel and get a room. But how would she get the dog inside without management knowing? The only thing that Heaven could do was leave the dog where she had found it. Once the room had been booked, she could then return and bring it back to her room, circumventing the hotel lobby. There, she could examine and see what the injuries were.

There was no time to waste. Again, Heaven reached inside the garbage bag and pulled out a tattered quilt. This should keep the dog warm until she could return and bring it inside. She walked in and asked for a room (the least inexpensive, she told the clerk). Heaven knew he was wondering if something fishy were taking place. She did not give him time to ask any questions. She paid cash for one night.

Money cannot buy happiness, but it can buy choices. Tonight's choice was to rescue that dog. She thanked the clerk and walked with haste to where she had left the dog.

She saw the spot. As she drew closer to the bush, Heaven could not hear anything. There was no whimpering. She whispered a prayer. She hoped she was not too late. She could not bear the thought of the dog dying in the bush all by itself.

CHAPTER 2

Brought back to the present by the whining of Malcolm, Heaven put Malcolm's treats inside the backpack and secured her personal items (wallet, keys, and cell phone). She was working on the matters at hand. Malcolm had become accustomed to this routine. Taking the wagon out of the back of the SUV, Heaven unloaded the snacks. The children loved the snacks. For some of the children, this would be the only food they would eat over the weekend until they returned to school on Monday.

Hunger did not discriminate. Heaven knew the feeling. School was the place where two meals a day could take place. Most elementary schools served a snack-type breakfast and then lunch. She only needed to remind herself of how she actually learned to count so efficiently. Heaven recalled the day with her Kindergarten teacher where Heaven questioned how many hours would go by from 2:00 p.m. until 9:00 a.m. the next morning, when Heaven would return to school. The teacher smiled and commented, "Eager to be in school?" The teacher told Heaven it would be 19 hours until she returned to school. The teacher did not have a clue that during those 19 hours away from school, Heaven would not eat.

Back to reality. Heaven kissed Malcolm on the top of the forehead. "Let's go deliver love and smiles." This was Heaven's favorite part – the delivery. The children and all the questions about Malcolm and what was in the bags and could they pet Malcolm were the highlights of the morning. As always, there were a few children who would begin trading once they dove into their snack bag. It was easy to see on their little faces which snacks were their favorites and which were not. The teachers did not like the "trading process". Afraid that someone may leave the school with less than what they started with or more of leaving empty-handed.

Heaven knew all of the children by first name or nickname. As each child made their way down the long line of tables where snacks had been placed, Heaven made sure that ONE of each item was placed in the bags the children had open. What made Heaven more empathetic to the plight of some of the children was that several would come back and request extra snacks for a younger sibling.

As the last child walked through the line and obtained his food, Heaven inhaled deeply. A drastic change needed to take place. She was going to need a facility to house her food donations, as well as an income to pay for the facility. Heaven looked over at Malcolm, who had been waiting patiently. He was curled in a ball. Sound asleep. The children with all their hugs and petting had worn him out. How he slept through the noise of the traffic and conversation of the children, Heaven did not have a clue. Heaven could not help but laugh at the picture before her. Malcolm had not a care in the world. This was as it should be. To sleep in peace and safety knowing that no harm would come your way.

She promised the children she would see them next Friday with some of the suggestions of new snacks they had given her. Heaven began the clean- up and stopped. Her feet were glued to the floor. Looking directly at her was the solution to her problems. She took a moment to re-read. Could she actually do it?

CHAPTER 3

Heaven and Malcolm arrived home. There was just enough time to feed Malcolm and then head to the bakery. She smiled. The bakery was her hiding place. Little did Heaven realize that the owner, TeeTee, would be the one to take her under her wing and show her the ropes of baking. TeeTee owned The Achy Bakery Heart. She was widely known in Windermere and surrounding counties for the best red velvet cream cheese cupcakes. "Sinful" is what most of the customers called the red velvet treat, all while licking their fingers. Heaven walked into the bakery. The smell and the aroma of baked cupcakes and donuts took her back in time to the first day she met TeeTee.

Heaven only had enough dollars to pay for the one night. She knew when she awoke, she would be homeless. She had been homeless before, but not longer than two or three days. Heaven was not just a survivor, she knew how to make her dollars stretch. And right now, the dollars needed to stretch like a rubber band. She looked around the room and gathered the garbage bag and then looked for the dog. What are the odds the hotel had such a unique name with the words "New View"? Kismet is what came to mind. Instances like this had occurred throughout Heaven's life. When she was younger, Heaven never gave a second thought to those moments. She shrugged them as they were – just moments. As she matured, there were too many "moments" that she could not ignore. There was no explanation other than the plain and simple fact, someone was watching over her.

Walking down the sidewalk that morning with Malcolm in tow (she had taken the yellow tie from the garbage bag to make a make-believe collar). She tied the garbage bag into a knot. Heaven had no clue as to the direction she should travel. But she felt drawn to where a crowd of people were gathered outside of a small store. As she drew closer to the crowd, she knew why there was a line. The smell of the bakery was wafting down the street. Even Malcolm was licking his chops. It was drawing folk from near and far. For the first time in a long time, Heaven genuinely smiled. She knew something extraordinary was about to occur.

CHAPTER 4

TeeTee saw the masses outside the bakery. Blessed was not even a word that could cover the success of the bakery. The town of Windermere supported her, not just financially, but with support and encouragement. Especially when she came up with a new idea for a cupcake.

As Heaven drew closer to the bakery, she did not want to leave Malcolm. They needed to remain together. They were a team. She made her way to the inside of the bakery with Malcolm. So far, so good. No one seemed to notice she had a huge dog attached to her hip. She observed the woman behind the counter. She greeted each customer by name. She asked how they were doing. She then told them quickly about the specials and asked for their order. She gave each individual the same amount of time and asked the same question over.

As the customers slid down to the cashier to pay, it was Heaven's turn. TeeTee smiled and said to the entire bakery, "It looks like we have two new members to add. Honey, what are your names?" Heaven lowered her head. She did not like to be the center of attention.

She slowly walked up to where the baked goods were featured. My name is Heaven Raye, and this is my best friend, Malcolm.

"Well, sugar, how can I help you and Malcolm? What's your flav of the day?" Heaven smiled. "I'll just have a glazed donut, please, ma'am." TeeTee watched as the young lady slid down to wait her turn to pay, along with her best friend, Malcolm. TeeTee noticed that Heaven Raye was rummaging through her backpack frantically. Malcolm was watching as well. Her hands were circling inside the backpack. TeeTee knew the next course of events.

TeeTee walked around from behind the counter. She pulled Heaven towards her into a small hug and whispered, "How about we call this order on the house, and if you can, we will work it off. Deal?" Heaven did not know what to say. She was not hungry, she was famished. She had not eaten since arriving in Windermere. Heaven had drank water, hoping that would keep her going until she could find…Heaven did not know what she needed to find. Before she could say "no", TeeTee reached for Heaven's hand and said "Why don't you and your best friend walk this way." Heaven was too tired to object. Both Heaven and Malcolm followed the woman called TeeTee. They walked past the cashier and into the back of the bakery. Before Heaven could ask any questions,

TeeTee opened the refrigerator. TeeTee was mumbling something about a sandwich for Malcolm and a salad of some kind for Heaven. Heaven laid her head down on the silver cooking counter. She did not mean to close her eyes. They were as heavy as rocks. Heaven needed just a few winks.

TeeTee turned around with food in hand for all. She looked at Malcolm. "Come here, big boy. Let's see if we can get you some water and a sandwich." Malcom did not move. He remained at Heaven's feet. "Okay, okay, I understand. You're her guardian angel. How about I bring it to you and you eat what you need?"

Malcolm did exactly what TeeTee knew he would do. He remained where Heaven was. She placed the water bowl down and tore the sandwich into tiny pieces. She watched as Malcolm ate and drank and then laid his head down. His eyes began to close. TeeTee winked at him. "You're safe here. I promise."

Heaven was disoriented. Where was she? Where was Malcolm? How long had she been asleep? The aroma brought her back to the present. The woman, TeeTee, and the bakery – Heaven was in the back of the bakery. She rubbed her eyes to clear the haze from them. Written in vibrant penmanship was a note that read, "Your companion has been fed. The food is for you, if needed. Take your time. When you're finished, your best friend will be fine back here. Come out and meet the staff."

Heaven took a bite of the turkey salad sandwich that was placed on a plate, along with potato chips, bottled water and the most exquisite cupcake Heaven had ever seen. It was too beautiful to eat. She took her time. She knew better than to scarf the food down. She looked at Malcolm, who was sitting alert. Heaven knew what he was waiting for – a crumb, anything to hit the floor. She tore a piece of the sandwich to give to Malcolm. He placed his paw on her leg as if saying, "thank you." Heaven leaned down and without even asking, Malcolm licked her. Heaven knew this was a moment of trust. She grabbed the sides of Malcolm's face and whispered, "You deserve the best things in the world."

Heaven washed her hands and walked through the doors to where the customers were chatting and the woman who had been so nice to Heaven and Malcolm, TeeTee. She was laughing and ringing up their orders. She did not miss a beat. Heaven had left Malcolm snoring. If Heaven were honest, this was a bit overwhelming. There was a lot of hustle and bustle to selling donuts and cupcakes. Heaven could tell that most of the customers were repeats. How else would TeeTee know EVERY single name of each?

TeeTee's eyes were drawn to the young woman who was doing her best to blend in behind the counter. She walked to where she was standing. "I've learned if you don't jump, then you won't know what's waiting for you on the other side." TeeTee reached underneath the counter and pulled out an apron. "Put this on, and let's get to working on that donut you owe me."

Heaven could not help but smile. Hanging on the back wall for all to see was the blackboard with the pricing. TeeTee called this "the cheat sheet". This is where "newbies" or new staff could take a quick glance if they could not memorize the entire board in one day. TeeTee twisted Heaven, so she could tie the apron. "My best advice is don't panic. You have something the customer is waiting for – the best sugar high ever." Heaven nodded. How difficult could it be to sell a few cupcakes and donuts for the day and pay kindness back with time?

CHAPTER 5

Heaven heard the clearing of a throat. She opened her eyes wide and turned in the direction of TeeTee. "Little girl, you have your head in the clouds. Tell me what's going on." Heaven cherished these moments with TeeTee. This was Heaven's time to bounce ideas off of TeeTee about the food pantry that Heaven wanted to establish. Heaven had held back on informing TeeTee of what she had found at the school that morning. Heaven did not know if she wanted to share the information with anyone just yet. She needed to ponder over this issue. She would do this after work. Heaven would do what anyone does when confronted with a dilemma with no answers in sight – make a "pros" and "cons" list. Didn't that always work?

The day had ended well. The store had never been empty. Heaven loved when the store was fast-paced. She looked at TeeTee and smiled. "I'm not daydreaming, but trying to figure out where I'm going to store the extra food needed to feed the kids. I need my own place. Everything is too expensive, and everyone wants what I don't have."

TeeTee tilted her head. It was going to be the same answer she had heard Heaven repeat for the past year – money. So, she would bite again. "And, what is it you don't have?" Heaven laughed. "Not even going to comment." TeeTee turned to her and hugged her. "I'll lock up the bakery. We had a good run today. We'll head over to the shelter. And then you can tell me what you haven't told me. Deal?"

"How, how do you know this—that I'm keeping something from you?" Heaven asked.

TeeTee locked the bakery door. "You've done nothing but fret all day. You gave a customer a cupcake when they asked for a donut. You forgot to put the icing on the red velvet cupcakes. And for some unknown reason, you keep scratching the right cheek of your butt. Just a few minor, but noticeable, details."

Heaven stopped. She reached for TeeTee's hand. "I do have something I need to share with you. I was going to wait, but now is as good a time as any. It was posted on the school's community bulletin board when I walked in this morning. I have had the paper crumpled in my jeans pocket all day. I wanted to be sure it was still there." Heaven pulled the paper and placed it in TeeTee's hand. "Read it and tell me what you think. Honest opinion. Don't hold back. I can take it." TeeTee laughed. "Okay, this sounds serious."

TeeTee unfolded the wadded paper and began to read. "As the Cookie or Cake Crumbles Bake-off Contest – Think you have the best cake, cookie or cupcake recipe? Then mark your calendar. Cash prize of $50,000 to overall baker(s) plus more prizes to be announced."

Heaven hesitated. "Think I have a shot? Even if I do not win the grand prize, did you see the cash prize of what the top three will receive? I don't need a lot, just enough to purchase a warehouse to store the donated food."

"Have you not learned anything I have taught you?" TeeTee inquired. "Anything is possible."

Heaven knew in her heart that TeeTee was right – anything was possible.

CHAPTER 6

As they were walking towards the homeless shelter, Heaven felt better. She hated keeping secrets from TeeTee. Approaching The Potters House Homeless Shelter, the line of individuals needing food was longer than normal. Daily, Heaven had noticed the increase in the distribution of meals. For some, this would be the only place that they would receive any kind of nourishment. Just as Heaven remembered, it would be a long wait until the individual would return the next day.

As she walked past the crowd, several knew her by name and called out to say hello. Heaven always made time to acknowledge each one.

In addition to the school, The Potter's House was one of two shelters where Heaven distributed food items. Had it not been for TeeTee and the bakery staff doing small fundraisers to bring awareness to the school and shelter, Heaven had no idea where the funds or items would have come from.

Heaven and TeeTee stopped and turned to the kitchen in order to get their aprons and gloves. It was a routine, and one that Heaven was grateful for. She hated change. Routine was key with her. Her friend, Bethanie, who volunteered with Heaven at the shelter, teased her about being dull and boring. It didn't bother Heaven. She hated drama. The more routine, the less drama.

Walking out of the kitchen to get stationed on the floor, Heaven stopped. This was not the same set of volunteers from last night. Bethanie saw Heaven stop and knew immediately what Heaven was thinking. She was frozen. Bethanie walked towards her. "Breathe. They are probably only here because they needed to be out and about in the community for public relations. You know and I know this happens all the time. It's more-than-likely a one-night stand." Heaven turned towards Bethanie and laughed. "That's a pretty fair analogy. Let's call it like the sports industry – one and done."

Heaven exhaled a sigh of relief. Once Bethanie, TeeTee, and Heaven got into their groove, all would be well. No need to get all fuzzy and warm with the new volunteers. Just be informative if they asked any questions. And before Heaven could panic, the evening would be over.

Bethanie remembered the first time she had met Heaven. Heaven came through the line to be served a meal. Bethanie noticed her immediately. Her big brown eyes and small frame and still manners thanking everyone that served her.

When Bethanie began to clean the table away from that evening's meal, Heaven stood up and began helping to clear away the tables. Bethanie winked at her and said "Remember to check underneath the tables, too. That's where I find all the napkins that have fallen to the wayside." As Heaven was leaving, Bethanie asked her if she would see her again. Heaven shrugged. Bethanie nodded and smiled. "We are here when you need us. I do hope to see you tomorrow." Bethanie watched as Heaven walked through the shelter's doors. She looked up and whispered, "Only you know her needs."

"Heaven, we have decided to place you as the lead to the line. You can be sure that all are served and if the servers/volunteers have any questions, you can answer them, since you, yourself, have been in this position." Heaven did not even hear one word Bethanie said. She was looking at the volunteers and assessing each. These were not the "typical" volunteers the shelter had. Heaven could tell these were "the corporate volunteers". None of them were dressed to get messy. All still had their white, long sleeve, cotton oxfords on with their ties still in place and their pressed khakis. And the shoes! What in the world were these volunteers thinking? Heaven shook her head and began to "tsk" with her tongue and grinned.

She had no idea that she was being watched until she heard him say, "Impressed are we?" Heaven looked up into the deepest blue eyes she had ever seen. Much more staring at him and she could drown in the intensity of the blue. For some unknown reason, the hair on her arms raised. She did not like his presumptuousness. He had no idea what Heaven was thinking, but she was getting ready to let him know. Who did he think he was? She tied her server apron tightly around her waist, which accentuated how small her waist was, and curtly replied: "Nope, I'm not impressed. It takes a lot to impress me. The only thing making a statement and drawing my attention to it is the fact that you're standing in my way. Other than that, nope, I'm not impressed."

Parker stepped back from the table. Who was this? Was she the shelter's manager? She was too young to own the building, let alone run the shelter. Parker had been surprised before, but not like this. Not with such disdain, and especially from a woman.

Parker's best friend leaned over to whisper in his ear. "Nice going. Not even here for five minutes and we are on her list." Parker turned and laughed. "Me? I didn't do anything except stand here and look volunteerish."

"Volunteerish? Is that even a word, or did you make it up because you screwed up and ticked off the person who is going to train us? Just apologize to her.

Tell her we are grateful to be here. Listen to what she says and let's get this evening over with," Alex nudged him with force to get his point across.

CHAPTER 7

Alex knew that Parker did not want to be here any more than he did. The email had been received this morning that the "monthly service opportunity" was today. Typically, the firm had enough individuals who would step up to the plate, and there was no need for Alex or Parker to show up. The firm received the PR, which was what made the partners happy. But today's email had been sent with "urgent reply" and that five additional volunteers would be needed. Before Alex could even intercom Parker, the managing partner knocked on his door, poked in his head in, and stated, "See you there tonight." It was not a question. It was a given statement. Parker knew he would need to make an appearance. For how long, that was another question. What made it even worse was the managing partner was his father. Parker did not have any leeway to tarnish the family name. There was a lot of pressure placed on him to be the successor to when his father stepped down for retirement.

As Parker was walking towards Heaven, she overheard the two men's conversation. She could not help but smile to herself. They were "greenhorns" to what the true meaning of volunteering entailed. TeeTee had told her when you give of yourself and your time, you give a thousand times over, plus it makes you feel good. She had quoted a Bible verse that Heaven had written on a piece of paper and kept in her wallet. It read, "Never forget, it is better to give than to receive. Acts 20:35." This had become Heaven's mantra. TeeTee had given this to her, and it had changed Heaven's life. Heaven wanted to do the same. She wanted to change the children's lives who worried about their next meal. In doing the research, Heaven had discovered that when a child is fed breakfast, more than likely, this child will be able to pay attention in school. Instead of losing focus on classes because the child is hungry and can only concentrate on that, being fed allows them to focus on their studies. It was quite easy and just too easy. Food was what was needed. It was required in the smallest of forms, but made the biggest impact for so many.

Heaven had promised the students and the school administration she would find a way to continue the donation of food to the children for the weekend. Now, if these gentlemen would pay attention to instruction, she could get home and begin the planning for the contest. She desperately needed a facility to make her dreams come true.

Parker had noticed the young woman with her arms crossed giving he and Alex a stern look with those pursed, pouty lips. Why "pouty" came to mind, he had no idea. He did not know who she was. He had yet to hear her name called, but instinct told him she had something to do with the shelter.

He walked towards the young lady and began with, "Let me apologize. Alex and I are ready…" And that was it. That was as far as he got before he received the hand in front of him. "Stop. No need to apologize. I just need to give you a few instructions and guidelines and then, you can be out of here just in time to do whatever it is that requires your attention. Are we good?"

Parker did not know whether to be pissed that SHE had just spoken to him like that or to laugh because she was not afraid to tell him off. The hand gesture was the best. No one had ever pulled a hand on him. It worked. It caught Parker off guard. "No need to get testy. Just tell us where we go, and we got you."

Heaven wanted to wipe that smug smile off his face, except she didn't know his name nor his friend's. She turned to the table that held the brochures, pamphlets, booklets, and the instruction guide to the shelter. She handed him a piece of paper. "There are only five rules that you must follow. If it's too difficult, please let me know now, and we will find someone else to take your spot."

Parker took the paper from her and read:

1 – At all times, please keep gloves on.

2 – At all times, serve the food with the utensils provided.

3 – At all times, if someone asks for help to carry their plate to the table, do so.

4 - At all times, please wear a smile.

5 – And last but not least, show the 3Cs.

Parker read it all. He got to number 5 and looked up at Heaven. "I know that you know we have no clue what #5 is. Are you going to tell us?"

"No," Heaven commented. "If you truly want to give back, then you'll stay and ask me at the end."

Parker was intrigued and pissed at the same time. Who in the world was this young lady? His father was walking towards Parker and Alex. "Everything good here? We are ready to roll out the red carpet on behalf of Pearl Edward Investments and show them how it's done. This will be a good public relations article for the business magazine, as well as the company's overall moral."

He had heard his father say this hundreds of times. But today, standing where he was, arguing with this beautiful volunteer, and she was beautiful – those words turned Parker's stomach.

CHAPTER 8

Heaven could not put her finger on it, but she was feeling "weird". After the conversation with the remaining volunteers, Heaven took her place in line. Better to place herself where she knew the action was going to be and that was right in between the two male volunteers whose smug smiles she wanted to wipe off their faces. She knew they recognized what she had done. Separate the forces to divide and conquer.

Heaven looked over at TeeTee and gave the nod. The doors opened. This was the part Heaven loved most. She enjoyed seeing the "regulars" come through the line. She knew at times, the regulars would bring a special guest or two. What made Heaven tear up at times was when the families would come through the line, mom, dad, children – all in need of food without being asked why or being judged. Oh, there were statistics that Heaven read and memos that the school would hand to her regarding the children's needs but when you got right down to it, folk were just plain ole hungry.

Heaven knew at any time, this could be her again. She was grateful for the blessing of this shelter. She had made a promise that no matter where her journey would take her, she would never forget the kindness she had received.

Heaven noticed that as each individual were approaching the line, they were a bit hesitant. It didn't dawn on Heaven until she heard Elwood say, "Might want to roll those pretty boy sleeves up, so ya don't get dirty." It was then that she knew why the shelter was so quiet and not the "norm". She stepped back and instructed all the corporate volunteers to please remove their ties and roll their sleeves up before another individual was served. Most turned to look at her with astonishment. Heaven took matters into her own hands. She turned towards Parker and pulled him towards her.

"Lawd, does no one understand, remove tie, roll sleeves. It's easy as 1-2-3. Watch me, please." Before Parker could even utter one word, she had unbuttoned his cuff sleeve and began to roll it up and then pushed it above his elbow for placement. She then repeated. She tippy-toed up and cocked her head sideways. "Going to help me or just stand there and hold the line up?" Parker noticed how her eyebrow drew up into a questioned arch. "No, no, I don't want the blame, nor your wrath."

"Then bend down, so I can remove your tie. They sure are not waiting on me." Why he acquiesced without even a comeback surprised Parker. He bent his head and felt her hands reach around his neck to lift the collar of his oxford shirt. Her fingers gently swept the side of his neck to pull the tie over his head. She caught her breath. She did not expect to react this way. Her words were captured in her throat. Her hands began to quiver. What was wrong with her? Looking up at him, she commented with the only words that came to mind, "There, was that so difficult? It didn't even hurt." Heaven did not need to be this close to him. He was having a strange effect on her. So, instead of pondering these feelings, she turned towards Parker's friend. He had already begun the disassembly of the tie and the rolling of the sleeves. "Good, now down to business," Heaven told them both.

Parker and Alex thought the line would never dwindle. There were so many. Alex looked at his friend and said, "I swear I've counted over 200 who have been fed. I had no idea this many were in need." They knew that the young lady who had trained them stepped away to begin the clean-up of the tables.

As they were completing their task of putting everything back in storage for the next day, Parker commented out loud, "I wonder who she is and what her story is?" Alex turned his head and laughed. "Didn't learn your lesson from the last one. Can we not just leave and know that we did a good thing tonight?

There's no reason to hang once we have finished what we were instructed to do."

"No. Remember what she told us. At the end of the event, we are to find her and ask about the three Cs. You're not curious to know?" Alex rolled his eyes. "No, I'm not, but I can tell by the tone of the statement, you are. Let's go find her so YOU can inquire about these three Cs."

As they were walking through the shelter, Parker was stopped by several volunteers, as well as individuals, he had fed that evening. He enjoyed chatting with them more than he cared to admit. At the office, chatting was not the "norm". Meetings and very long conferences were the protocol. This was a nice diversion. Moving in and out of the people and the tables, Parker kept searching for "her". He had inquired about her whereabouts. Each told him that she probably needed to leave with her mother in order to get to work early at the bakery. It was as if she were a ghost. She vanished into thin air. Why did this bother him? Why did he need to see her? Why did the three Cs become important to him?

CHAPTER 9

Heaven was pleasantly surprised that they both had stuck it out. She figured an hour into serving and getting splattered with food, they would make an excuse to leave. Typically, that's how most new volunteers reacted. Why should he or his friend be any different? As the evening wore down, Heaven observed the man who gave her a "weird" feeling. Maybe weird was not the right choice. Heaven knew she felt different around him.

He was muscular. She could tell through his shirt. He had a long torso. His height was about six feet. Overall, he was handsome. But what made Heaven want to learn more was the fact he was not your average corporate volunteer. His ears were pierced. He had long, blondish-brown hair that had been slicked back into a straight ponytail. His hair was thick. His eyes were jet set blue with a speckle of black. When he looked at her, purpose was written in those eyes. Heaven shook her head. Lawd, did he notice she had been staring at him?

Heaven remembered her last statement to him and his friend, "At the end, come see me and I'll tell you." As Heaven cleaned away the food and plates from the table, she recalled that she could not stay. She could not share with them what she intended. Malcolm. She wanted to be with Malcolm, at home in bed watching a movie, where all would be safe and normal.

Heaven sensed that tonight was a changing point in her life. Something was going to happen. All her life, she could sense when the wind would change direction and take her down another path. She felt that tonight.

She arrived home, parked, and walked up the sidewalk. She could hear him on the other side. Heaven did not know, but for whatever reason, Malcolm always knew when it was her. She unlocked the door, and before she could even open, Malcolm had pushed his way around and jumped on her with such exuberance, Heaven braced herself to get inside. "Hold on, hold on. Let me lay everything down, change, and we'll go for a 'you know what.'" She kissed Malcolm on his cold nose, walked to the bedroom, and changed into her sweats and tennies. Malcolm was watching. Heaven knew he was counting the routine down.

The key that triggered Malcolm that walking was on the agenda was when Heaven went to the basket where Malcolm's toys and leash were stored. He began jumping around and running in a circle. It was more difficult to get the leash on him than to walk him. She could barely get him to stand still to place the leash over the top of his head and snap it. She laughed. Heaven loved walking just as much as Malcolm. It allowed her time to check off the day's events and plan for tomorrow's to do list.

They returned from their walk. Malcolm, out of routine, went for the water first. Heaven knew there would be more water on the floor than in the water dish. It was okay. She did not mind. Malcolm was her safety net. When her days were filled with anxiety and trepidation, just knowing that Malcolm would be home waiting for her kept her calm.

The second best thing in her life to keep her motivated was baking. In the time she had been working for TeeTee and now with TeeTee, Heaven felt confident in her skills as a baker. She looked at Malcolm. "What do you think, strawberry cheesecake cupcakes or angel food cake? Either way, we will take it in with us and see what the boss says." Malcolm tilted his head. "Yep, that's what I thought, too. Let's bake both." As Heaven began to pull out the pans and the ingredients, she could not get him out of her mind. Who was he? Had he tried to find her? She would never know. She doubted she would ever see him again or volunteering at the shelter for that matter.

CHAPTER 10

Walking into work, Parker was determined to find out about the young woman at the shelter. He could not fathom why she was still on his mind, but she was. He had asked several of the individuals that evening at the shelter if they knew where she had gone or where he might be able to find her. They were as tight-lipped as a one-year-old toddler with something in his mouth that he knew he shouldn't have.

There was a moment, though. An elderly gentleman came up to Parker as he was walking back to his car and said, "If you are looking for Heaven, you just need to look up," and pointed his finger towards a bright light, showcasing the words "Achy Bakery Heart". Parker winked at the elderly man and shook his hand. "Thank you." The gentleman looked at him and grinned, "Just don't tell her I told you."

Parker felt different as he arrived at the office. The elevator doors opened, and he could hear Vivian, their receptionist, greeting staff. He stopped at Vivian's desk. "Good morning, Viv. I need you to do me a quick favor. Can you send an email out that a meeting will be held with all staff in the large conference room promptly at 10:00 a.m.?" He wanted to be sure that everyone knew how much he appreciated their time given last night to the shelter.

The meeting went well. Parker could tell by everyone leaving that they were taken by surprise. He literally could see sighs being released. Parker did not think he was an ogre or a hard knocks kind of boss, but evidently, his staff did. That was about to change. He thanked each one and informed them to be on the lookout for the next volunteer adventure.

He shook his head. He truly had perplexed his staff. He could only imagine the talk at the water cooler. First and foremost, who was he and what had happened to their boss? Parker felt good. He liked changed. The unknown. Shaking things up kept everyone excited and fresh for the next big adventure.

Now, if he could muster up the courage for his next leap of faith. Travelling to the bakery. Lord, what was the name again? Oh, yes – The Achy Bakery Heart.

Parker checked his calendar. Clients would not be in until late afternoon. No one would miss him. No one would realize he was gone. Screw it. He had to know who she was.

He pushed the down button on the elevator and looked back at Viv. "I have a few errands and outside appointments. I should return no later than 2:00 p.m. should anyone ask, okay?" The good thing about this statement was Viv was on the telephone and could only nod in agreement.

The drive to the address given for The Achy Bakery Heart was approximately a 30-minute drive. It could not be that close. Why had he not heard of the bakery before. The staff was always bringing in delectables from bakeries. This one, as far as he could remember, was not on his radar.

Parker enjoyed the ride. One corner to turn and he would be there. As he was turning right from the stop sign, he noticed out of the corner of his eye what he knew was the bakery. On top of the building was a broken heart, split in two pieces, embedded in a cupcake. Could this day get any better? Now he knew why it was called The Achy Bakery Heart. Behind every name is a story. This one should prove interesting.

CHAPTER 11

Where were they coming from? This day was no different than the rest. It was just National Angel Food Cake Day. That was the reason she had made the delightful dessert last night. She wanted not only to surprise TeeTee, but to showcase her baking skills with their patrons. Heaven had been complimented many times, by the regulars, on many occasions. She never took them seriously, but always gave a polite thank you.

The door kept swinging open, and the customers did not stop. Heaven and TeeTee had no time to come out from the back to see if Ginny and Sarah were holding their own. As fast as they could, they were baking more cupcakes with their special crème frosting. The only thing Heaven was sure of was that the patrons loved her samples she had placed out this morning. Heaven could hear their comments as their purchases were finalized. "Great job. Love the samples. Thank you for your kindness." And then, she overheard a voice that sounded all-too-familiar. It made the hairs on her arm raise and heart began to race. "There's something missing."

Parker entered the bakery to be thrust into the line of patrons. He neared the counter, and noticed the silver plate on top of the counter, displaying the samples. He drew closer. It cannot be. He cannot believe it. The last time he had a bite of this dessert, it was with his mother. He reached to take a sample. Placing it inside his mouth, the memories came flooding back. He did not mean to, but it was heard by several patrons. "There's something missing."

Before he could finish his thought or enjoy the memories, the swinging doors to the back of the bakery flew open. "I'm sorry. Who said that?" There was no turning back. And even if Parker wanted to, one of the customers who had just taken a bite, turned and pointed his finger at him. "He did, Heaven."

So that was her name. Heaven. AND he had just commented on what he knew was going to be his demise – her angel food cake. Parker looked around at the customers, hoping to see a smiling face. There was no one. "You just put yourself in the center of a big ole pot hole," the man winked. "Everyone, let's take seat. This morning is getting ready to be a wing-dinger."

Heaven looked at her favorite customer. "Stop, I'm not going to thrash him too much. Just need to bring him down a notch or two." He hugged her and whispered. "He's new to the group. Don't be too hard on him. You want him to come back. Looks as if he could purchase the entire store and not blink an eye."

"I don't care if he had a million dollars and found me a warehouse to store my food for the children, THERE IS NOTHING MISSING from the recipe."

The rest of the customers turned to watch the conversation that was about to take place. Everyone in the bakery knew Heaven or knew of Heaven. This poor guy was in for a rude awakening. They did not want to miss this. Plus, several were actually curious as to what was missing from the angel food cake.

Heaven came from behind the counter. The hair on her arms was still raised. What was going on? It hit her like a ton of bricks. This was him. This was the volunteer at the shelter. He was standing in the bakery. She walked around from the counter. "I don't know your name. I don't need to know your name. What makes you think something is missing from the angel food cake? Are you a baker? Do you own your own bakery?"

Parker didn't want to admit it, but this woman, called Heaven, intrigued him. She was standing in front of him, dressed in her apron, covered in flour, with hands on her hips, oozing indignance.

She began pointing her finger near his chest. His Henley shirt showcased how muscular he was. Heaven's finger felt on fire. Good grief. She pulled back and started with, "Look here, Mister Smarty Pants, I don't know who you are. I don't want to know. When I ask you the ingredient that YOU think is missing, you better be dang skippy sure you know what you're talking about."

There was something about her frustration being taken out on him that made him want to know more. But there really was something missing from the angel food cake. How could he approach the subject with tact and not tick her off even more than what she was displaying at this moment? From the look of consternation written on Heaven's face, he needed to tread lightly. Plus, he had an entire audience standing and watching his every move.

"How about we talk in private?" Parker angled his head toward the back. Heaven did not know whether to laugh or to actually invite him to the back. He had no idea what was behind that door. She chose the first. "Scared are you? Do you really know what is missing, Mr.? What is your name, please?" Heaven inquired sarcastically.

Parker smiled. She was not going to make this easy. Fine, he was curious about this young woman, and this little tit-for-tat disagreement was not going to deter him. Before she had time to respond or change her mind for that matter, Parker placed his hand on her elbow and guided her towards the back (or at least what he thought was the back). Please let it be the back, he thought to himself.

TeeTee was watching the exchange. As Heaven walked by, TeeTee mouthed, "If you need me, scream." Heaven smirked. Need her. It was more as if he would need TeeTee when he encountered what or who was in the back. Heaven returned the statement with an "I got this." TeeTee gave her the thumbs up and returned the attention to her customers. This gentleman was in for a world of hurt. She would love to be a fly on the wall.

CHAPTER 12

Arriving in the back of the bakery, Parker dropped his hand from Heaven's elbow. He sensed, rather than saw, the security guard that was bearing his teeth. It had become routine for Malcolm to arrive with Heaven at the bakery. Sometimes, the day got away and was extended. She did not like crating Malcolm and leaving him home for so long. The next best thing was to bring him.

TeeTee did not have a problem with Malcolm as their security for the bakery. In fact, the employees commented it was good for business, as well as morale for the staff. A special spot had been designated for Malcolm to rest, sleep, and keep one eye open. There had been times where all had been in the back and Malcolm's keen sense of hearing would alert them to the fact that someone had walked through the doors. Of course, the bell attached to the door helped, too.

Parker froze in his tracks. "You knew he was back here. Admit it?"

Heaven laughed. "Of course, I did. He rescued me. His name is Malcolm, and he is very protective of not just me, but the staff also."

"Fine, fine, I get it," Parker smiled.

Heaven watched as Malcolm walked towards Parker. She knew what was going to happen. Malcolm sniffed Parker with hesitation. It would only take a second for Malcolm to make his mind up about the individual in front of him. Heaven knew the outcome she was looking for. She was sure Malcolm would see right through this man. But instead, Malcolm took his head and pushed into Parker's hand.

Parker exhaled. "Well, I've passed the first test. What else ya got?"

Heaven shook her head and looked at Malcolm. "Traitor," she whispered under her breath and then rubbed the back of Malcolm's head. Malcolm seemed satisfied that nothing was amiss and Heaven was not in danger. He walked to his bed and plopped down. Parker did not want to admit it. He was a bit worried when he first saw the dog. Parker knew Alex would not believe this story. Shoot, Parker could not believe how this day was unfolding.

Heaven turned around to be sure that Malcolm was asleep. Just like that, he was snoring. She did feel a bit better about the man standing in front of her. Heaven knew that Malcolm would protect her.

Parker watched the display of emotion come across Heaven's face. He could tell that Heaven had a special bond with the dog. And what a name. Who names their dog Malcolm? Before he could actually inquire about the name, Heaven cleared her throat. "Okay, Mr. Know It All, down to business. I'm waiting with baited breath. Since you seem to consider yourself a baker, pray tell, what ingredient is missing?" Heaven questioned him.

If only Parker could kiss that sassy smile off her face. This was the first time he took time to truly look at the young lady standing before him. She was petite in size. Her eyes were almond-shaped. Her smile was infectious, even with the indignant look she was attempting. Her fingers did not possess the fake fingernails so many women at the office wore. Her apron strings had been tied around her more than once. She had done this the night at the shelter, too.

Parker heard a loud cough and then heard Heaven state the obvious, "Are you staring at my cupcakes or what?"

Parker could not help it. He busted out laughing. "Your what? And for the record, the ingredient missing is..."

Heaven could not believe her ears. No, he did not just say the word "missing".

"Well, I'm not 'Mr. Know it All', but you can call me Parker. My name is Parker Stevens. And I'm going to venture to say that cream of tartar was not added?"

Who was this man? She was in trouble. Just by using the words "cream of tartar", Heaven knew that he was familiar with baking. How good he was at baking had yet to be established, but only individuals who "baked"—and not "cooked"—would know what this ingredient was. She had to rethink back to last night. Did she skip the cream of tartar? Did she even have cream of tartar in her home? Was cream of tartar necessary? Lord, she was going to have to inform him he was right. Heaven did not like to be wrong. More than that, he was correct.

Parker watched her face. He could tell she was thinking if she had included cream of tartar. Her faced revealed that she had not. The ball was in his court. He could be cocky about this fact or he could offer to help her bake an angel food cake with the cream of tartar included. Before she could say anything, he commented, "I don't mind baking an angel food cake with you, to show you my skills. That's if you have the time."

Heaven looked at Parker Stevens. He could have said "told you so", but he didn't. He wanted to bake with her. Why was she feeling that her cheeks were turning red? This man, since meeting him at the shelter, had not left her mind. And now, here he was standing in the back of TeeTee's bakery with her. Were the walls closing? The room was feeling very small. The space between Heaven and Mr. Stevens became very constrictive. Heaven could not breathe. Ninety-nine percent of the time, Heaven could tell what had been baking in the back. This moment, she could only sense the masculinity of Mr. Stevens and his proximity to her.

Heaven stepped back. She did not realize that several bowls were still on the counter. What was even worse, a few of the bowls still had a bit of dribblings inside. Parker caught her eye as she turned her head to see what she had backed into. If he didn't grab her, she was going to be covered in God knew what.

Without hesitation, he reached around her waist and pulled her into his chest. "I got you. From the looks of it, none too soon." He looked at the young woman and remembered she had not shared her entire name. Parker looked into her eyes, while she was in his embrace. "What is your full name?" The only thing Heaven could do to balance herself, without falling further into his chest, was place both her hands on his chest. Big mistake. Huge mistake. Her hands were on fire. Did he have a fever? Is that why he was hot to the touch? Was she coming down with something?

Heaven looked up. She was falling into those eyes. They were bluer than blue. She could not muster the one word he had requested. Her name. Not only did her hands not want to leave him, her voice had left her as well. In all of her 25 years, she had never felt this way. Anxious, nervous, and shy – all rolled into one. She bit her bottom lip. Should she tell him?

Parker saw her hesitation. When she bit her bottom lip, he wanted to rub his thumb across those lips. He barely knew this young lady, and yet, he sensed something. Somehow, her presence was causing him to have thoughts he should not be having.

"Cat got your tongue? I am quite serious when I tell you that I will offer my services to bake with you, especially the angel food cake. I promise not to critique until we pull it out of the oven."

TeeTee walked through the doors from the front counter to the back, all the while talking to herself. Heaven knew what she was up to. This was TeeTee's way of alerting her that she was on her way.

Heaven nodded. "No, that's okay. I think I will try the recipe by myself. Maybe you could return another day to test the samples?"

"Afraid of a little competition?" Parker teased her. He knew she would take the bait. She would not back down. Instinct told him that she was different than most of the women he had flirted with or dated. "Just so you know, my mom taught me how to bake. Angel food cake was one of her favorite recipes. If you're too busy, we can bake at the shop after close of business. We both know our commitment will be less than two hours."

How could Heaven tell him? She was not scared of him. She was scared of how he was making her feel. Right now, baking would be the easy part. Working with him, side by side, seemed a bit dangerous. Heaven stepped out of his reach just as TeeTee walked in. "Everything good in here? I need you back out front, sweetie."

Heaven nodded. "I'll be right there."

Parker realized this was his cue. But he did not want to leave without knowing her full name and without her agreement to bake with him. "I tell you what, Heaven, when I get off work, I will swing over and see how busy the bakery is, and we can rally together to bring the customers the best angel food cake in the morning. Sound like a plan?"

A plan? They were planning now. Things were moving too fast. Heaven did not have time to negate his self-invite. She needed to be on the floor. "Fine. We close at 5:00 p.m. If you want, feel free to swing by, and we will bake the angel food cake your way." This should be his cue to turn around and leave.

Instead, he left with a smile and statement of, "I promise, you won't regret it."

Parker walked towards the swinging door and allowed Heaven to go first. Several of the customers were still inside, seated at the small tables and chairs. Heaven heard Mr. Welby make the statement, "Well, he's still standing. That's a positive." Parker even overheard him. He looked at Heaven and winked. "You have a huge village protecting you. Remind me not to upset Mr. Welby." Heaven laughed. "He's harmless. He just cares about folks."

"That, I can tell. One of those folks he cares a lot about is you. I will see you tonight after 5:00 p.m. Be ready to be baked off your feet." And just like that, Parker Stevens had walked out of the bakery.

CHAPTER 13

Parker pulled into his parking spot at work. He did not open the door. Only a few hours left until he was to return to the war zone...or the bakery. Either way, he was looking forward to returning. He walked in and saw his best friend. Alex looked at him, smiled, and said, "Dare I ask what you did for lunch? Because the way you're smiling, I need to know who she was." Parker shook his head. "What makes you think it was a she?" His friend of more than 15 years, Alex, laughed. "No one comes back from lunch with a smile as big as you have, unless something special took place. So, share. Who was she?"

Parker could not resist. He did not know why, but he could not stop smiling as he was telling Alex about the bakery encounter and seeing the young woman from the shelter. He ended the story with "and oh yeah, I am baking with her tonight after work." Parker turned away and headed towards his office. He looked over his shoulder. Alex was standing there with his mouth wide open. He didn't know what to say. He could see Parker laughing as he closed his office doors.

Heaven could not stop watching the clock. In just 30 minutes, it was going to happen. He was going to walk through those bakery doors. What had she gotten herself into? TeeTee had told her that her competitiveness was going to get her in a pickle. She admired Heaven for her go-give spirit. TeeTee understood Heaven's drive to succeed. It was not to be better than anyone. It was that Heaven needed to give back. It was in her nature.

Heaven looked at the clock again. She could hear the second digital hand. Heaven needed to prepare the back with the ingredients they would need. There was no way he knew all the ingredients necessary for angel food cake. Plus, he was a man. She had yet to meet anyone, and especially this man, who could make angel food cake better than Heaven. Better yet, he looked as if dirt had never hit his body. He was just too clean.

TeeTee walked in the back. She watched as Heaven laid the ingredients out in the order they would be placed in the mixing bowl. TeeTee would have enjoyed taking credit for Heaven's baking skills, but that was not the case. It was an innate ability. Heaven was just born to be a baker. Anyone could mix ingredients as they were listed in a recipe, but only a few individuals could take a recipe and make it better. TeeTee had always told Heaven, "Before you present the cookie, the cake, or even the donut to a customer, you must taste it. If you like it, then it's guaranteed the customer will. If you don't like it, start again until you do."

Heaven was placing the mixing bowls, measuring cups, utensils, and ingredients on the baking counter. She didn't hear TeeTee walk in. As Heaven was laying the eggs out, TeeTee came to the side and did her little *tsk, tsk* noise. "Baby girl, you better be on your A-game. I'm pretty sure this young man knows a bit about baking. Maybe not as much as you, but enough for you to be cautious." She winked at Heaven. "Remember to set the alarm before you leave. I'll see you in the morning." She hugged Heaven and whispered, "Be nice to him. Don't scare him away. You never know... he could be the one."

Heaven hugged TeeTee. "I'll play nice. Can you take Malcolm home for me? I know he does not want to be here any longer than necessary." TeeTee called for Malcolm to come. Heaven knew TeeTee would take great care of Malcolm. Heaven needed to be alert. No distractions.

The bakery was empty. Everything was clean and ready for the morning patrons. Only one thing left to do.

Heaven was pacing in the back. The clock had not moved for ten minutes. She knew that was a lie. He would be here in ten minutes. What had she done? She must be slipping. Since her arrival into to the small town of Windermere, Heaven did not have the time, nor did she make the time, for any personal relationship with the opposite sex. Yet, in less than ten minutes, he was going to be at the front entrance of the bakery. She felt nauseated. She was going to throw up. She was going to pass out. Much more thinking like this and she was going to leave. She giggled anxiously. Oh joy, the giggle. The goofy giggle had returned.

She walked to the front of the bakery to check to see if he was standing outside. He was. His back was to the door. It seemed he was preoccupied with something or someone. She could tell he was on his cell phone. She could also surmise that the conversation was a bit heated. As she was unlocking the door and he was turning around, the last words she heard would resonate with her for a while, "I don't care what you say, I'm here. We will discuss this in the morning."

Heaven turned the lock, and Mr. Parker Stevens jerked around as if he had been shot. "I was checking to see if you might have arrived, and here you are. I did not mean to startle you," Heaven smiled.

Her smile was all that he needed. He forgot about those last words with his father. He would deal with him in the morning at the office. Right now, his entire focus was on her. "It's nothing. It will wait until morning.

Are you ready for your baking lesson?" He saw her eyebrow go up and knew he had hit a nerve. Good. Now, his direction could turn toward what he truly enjoyed – baking. Only the closest of his friends knew about his hidden talent. And some had actually been afforded the opportunity to taste test some of Parker's extraordinary talents.

Heaven laughed. "A bit full of yourself this evening, aren't you? Don't answer. It does not matter. We are on equal playing ground, because neither of us knows what the other is capable of."

Parker could not resist. "You have no idea, Heaven, what I am capable of. But I can honestly guarantee, you will not be disappointed." He stepped towards Heaven to gain access inside. They were so close, you could not place a whisper between them.

"Heaven…..Heaven…..are you going to allow me to come inside?" Parker waited. Heaven's beautiful eyes were fixated on him. "Never mind. I got this." Parker put his arm around her waist as if he were dancing with her. He turned her, so that he was actually inside the bakery, all the while not removing his arm. Heaven inhaled. He felt the rise of her breast against his chest. If he did not release her soon, she was going to feel the rise of him. His body had never betrayed him like this. He was always in control.

Heaven cleared her throat. "Yes, yes. I'm sorry. Come on in. Let me lock the door behind us. You know where the baking area is in the back. I just need to check a few things. I'll be there in five." Heaven watched his back as he retreated to where they would bake. It hit her like ranch dressing and fries go together – she was going to be close to him. His scent as he walked past Heaven was one of sandalwood. He was wearing a pink Henley long sleeve shirt. The blue jeans accentuated his "assets". His hair was down. It was long and thick. Not like when she had seen him before. He had kept it knotted. He was a tall drink of water next to her. Walking to the back, she admitted to herself, he was sexy and she was in trouble.

Parker noticed she had laid all the ingredients as well as the bowls and utensils out that would be needed. He double-checked everything. She did remember the cream of tartar. He smiled to himself. She was thorough. He loved that. He only needed to worry about her and the proximity of where he placed himself. She walked from behind and handed him an apron. "Here ya go. Let me know if you need help with anything." Parker turned and looked at her as she was putting her apron on over her head. He knew she would need to double knot her apron. Her waist was small. He watched as she fumbled with the strings to pull them around again to the front of her waist.

Good grief. Why could she not tie the strings to the front of her waist? For some unknown reason, her hands were shaking. There was no cause for this other than one fact. It was him. Heaven told herself there was no need to worry. How good could he be a better baker? Then, she thought to herself, *That's what I'm worried about. He could be better than me.* Before she could attempt a second try at tying the apron strings, he was in front of her. He reached around and pulled the strings forward and tied a perfect bow to hold the apron in place. His hands were still at the bow. He was not removing his hands. Heaven placed her hands on his to remove them. His touch made her burn. She felt her entire body begin to react. This feeling was new to her. A want that was coursing through her veins.

Heaven quickly commented, "We don't have a lot of time, you ready?" He watched her reaction to his touch. It was a good thing she did not notice his reaction to her. He had been in relationships, but something told him she was different. She licked her lips in anxiousness, not realizing what Parker's mind was imagining. Parker could not reveal the effect she was having on his concentration. Better to focus on the task at hand, which was that mixing bowl and placing the ingredients inside.

He took in each step she began. She's good. Very precise and methodical with the process. Without thinking, Parker came up behind her and placed his arms around her. Heaven could not breathe. She placed all the ingredients in the bowl and picked the spoon up to mix the ingredients. Parker could not resist. He placed his hand on hers and began the circular motion with her. The motion was slow. Heaven stopped. "It looks divine," he whispered into Heaven's ear. She could not go any further. Something was happening. She was in foreign territory. She grabbed Parker's hands, without realizing her hands were covered in flour and sugar.

Heaven began to try to shake off the flour and sugar. All this did was enhance her senses to his touch. Parker, even if he wanted to, could not move from her gentle embrace of sweeping the ingredients from his hands. How this one gentle motion took a turn, Parker had no idea. He only knew that he needed to see her face. He turned Heaven towards him. He touched her nose with his finger and left a small patch of flour and sugar.

CHAPTER 14

Heaven did not know why, but she felt the need to return the favor. She turned and reached inside the mixing bowl and sprinkled a bit of flour, just like a fairy would do with magic sprinkle dust. "There now, we both match," Heaven inhaled breathlessly. He reached around her and placed in his hands into the batter. He turned and marked each side of her cheeks.

"Much better," Parker told her. Heaven could not believe he had actually done that.

"Oh, not quite, but it will be," Heaven giggled. She took some of the batter and playfully flung at Parker. It hit him square in the chest.

"Oh, it's game on, Heaven. You better run." Parker grabbed a handful of the batter and threw it up in the air and grabbed Heaven quickly before she knew what his motive was. Before she could react, they both were covered in angel food cake batter.

Looking at her, he felt the sexual tension in the room. He wondered if she did. There was no way she could deny the attraction. Before he could ask, he did what any man who was holding a beautiful woman covered in cake batter would do – he kissed her. Time stopped as his lips met hers.

Heaven's heart was pounding in her chest. Her knees became weaker. Her focus was only on how soft his mouth felt against hers. He had invaded all her senses. It was him and only him that her attention was being given. She had sensed the change in Parker. She was still not clear if she had dreamed this moment, but when his hand curled around her neck to pull her closer, she could not refuse. The warm feeling of her breath against his lips was too inviting.

Parker stepped back. He could tell by the flush of her cheeks that Heaven was feeling the heat of her emotions. He did not want to stop. He looked at her and placed his thumb under her chin and whispered, "Heaven, look at me. I did not come here to do this. Since the first time I saw you at the shelter, I have wanted to kiss you. Do you want me to stop?"

Heaven could not believe what she was hearing. Her body was tingling. She was floating. Her feet were not touching the floor. The feel of his body touching hers was like a fire burning that could not be put out. It was all she could do not to melt into his embrace.

Heaven shook her head no. "No, Parker, I do not want you to stop. Please don't stop." Before he could change his mind, Heaven reached for his hands and brought them to her heart. "My heart is racing. I cannot stop it. I do not want you to stop." Parker pulled her in, claiming her mouth again. Heaven moaned a throaty sound. Parker rubbed Heaven's bottom lip. They were swollen and pouty with desire. "Heaven, you deserve the very best."

Heaven had not allowed herself to dream of moments such as this. This moment was not real. He could not be real. And yet, here he stood in front of Heaven. She blinked. He did not disappear. His hands untied her apron. He pitched it to the side. This allowed him the access he so desperately desired. His fingers moved to explore what was under Heaven's blouse. He felt her draw a breath. This only helped to accentuate the tininess of her frame. He curled his hands around her waist. His thumbs began a circular motion on each side of her waist. They had a mind of their own and reached Heaven's bra. He reached around, and with one silent twist, Heaven's bra had been opened.

His hands found what they had been exploring and could not find. The nipples of Heaven's breasts were taut. Heaven arched her back, so Parker could have easier access. A circular motion and then a gentle tug was all that was needed for a groan of satisfaction to leave Heaven's lips. But this was not enough. Parker slowly raised her blouse and bra. He kissed one breast and then the other.

Each deserved his attention. He suckled each nipple until she moaned in ecstasy. He moved lower down to her belly and placed kisses along the way.

Her belt was in the way. He looked up at her. She was balancing herself by holding on to his shoulders. He began to unbuckle her belt. Heaven inhaled deeply. This allowed Parker quicker access to shimmy her jeans down to her feet. He ran his hands slowly up the sides of her legs. He cupped the back of her derrière. Heaven was going to pass out. Nothing prepared her for the heat that was rising between her legs.

Parker's fingers slowly slid underneath Heaven's panties. His attention was drawn to the fact that they were covered in paw prints. Who was this young woman? Heaven bit her bottom lip and moaned. What was he doing? Why was he doing this to her?

"Parker, I can't. I don't know what you want me to do." Parker looked up.

"Ssshhh, it's okay. If you don't like what I'm doing, tell me."

She nodded her head. She did not have the will to speak. As Parker moved his way up, Heaven held tightly to Parker. She did not want to let him go. She reached to pull his shirt over his head. That was a big mistake. Huge mistake. He was not just fit, he was perfect. She put her hands on his chest. He placed his hand over hers and moved it down to his belt. Heaven unbuckled and unzipped his pants. Heaven could not take her eyes off of Parker. She saw the effect she was having on him. His desire was felt against her skin. "Trust me?" Parker whispered. She nodded.

"Open your legs for me, please." Heaven did. Parker's finger teased the outer lip until he felt her body react with moistness. Slowly, he inserted his finger inside and felt Heaven contract. Heaven's body betrayed her. It began to respond to the rhythm of Parker's finger. Just when she thought she could not take any more, Parker began to rub his manhood against her. Heaven knew there was something else. More. She needed more. There was an emptiness that had yet to be fulfilled. She did not want to tell him that she was a virgin. She did not want him to know how inexperienced she was.

Heaven pulled Parker closer. "I do not know why, but I need to feel you, Parker. There is an ache, and I know only you can make it go away. Please make it go away." Parker looked at Heaven for the first time. Vulnerable and honest.

CHAPTER 15

He pulled back. "Open your eyes, Heaven. I cannot. I cannot believe I am going to say this." Parker began to pull his boxers and then pants back up. He zipped and buckled them. He reached down and pulled Heaven's jeans back up. He did just as he had done with his – zipped and buckled. He reached for her bra and t-shirt. "Raise your arms for me, Heaven." He placed the bra through her arms, and clasped it. He then placed the t-shirt over her head and pulled down. He kissed her shoulder and turned her around to face him.

"Let's finish the job. Let's bake that angel food cake. Agreed?" Heaven was in disbelief. He acted as if nothing had happened. Fine, two could play this game.

"Yes, by all means, let's finish the job." And that is what happened. They began separating the ingredients and then placing what was needed in the bowl. The blender was ready. The mold had been prepped to pour the mixture into. Sugar, cake flour, cream of tartar, salt, vanilla extract, and egg whites – the simplest of ingredients that would turn into the most incredible dessert.

Parker acted as if nothing happened. He had to. She did not know if she should broach the subject of what just happened 15 minutes ago or continue as if nothing had occurred. Either way, she was enjoying herself. He was very knowledgeable about baking. This made Heaven happy. She felt Parker cared about the process and the outcome of baking.

Parker was observing her. She was pondering her next move. He could tell by her pursed lips. She was analyzing each step. Why could he not have finished what he started? What stopped him? This was the second time meeting her, so there were no attachments yet. And then it hit him like a ton of bricks. That word "yet". He wanted to pursue these feelings he was having for Heaven. He did not want to rush in too head strong and scare her away.

Heaven could feel his eyes on her. She genuinely wanted to know where he learned to bake. The safest option was to ask this particular question and not pursue the whys or ifs of what had just occurred. As she was cleaning the counter, she thought, *There is nothing to lose by asking.* "Parker, I know that most men can cook, but not all men can bake. Where did you learn the craft of baking?"

Parker grinned. He loved to tell the story. As Heaven stated, most men can cook, but not all men could bake. "My mom taught me, Heaven. I would bake with her when I was little. As soon as I was big enough to stand on the stool and reach the counter, she would bake with me. She was known for her angel food cake. Not just the baking, but also the decorations that she applied to the cake. I am an only child, so she smothered me with attention of what she loved to do in the hopes that I would love it, too. And guess what? I do. I love to bake. And now you. Where did you learn to bake?"

"TeeTee taught me. I know that the good Lord led me to TeeTee and the Achy Bakery Heart. What she gave me was not just the knowledge but time. No matter how long was needed to finish a dessert, we stayed until it was completed. Time, Parker. She gave me time. There is never enough time in the day to do everything, but you can do a little."

Parker glanced her way. That was pretty profound. There was more to Heaven than met the eye. He wanted to know more. He needed to know more about Heaven Raye. Parker heard the timer go off. "This is it. Make or break time."

Both slowly walked to the industrial oven, as if walking on glass. Heaven looked at Parker. Parker looked at Heaven. Both burst into laughter. "You nervous, too, Heaven?" Heaven nodded.

"Not as much as you should be. I know I can bake. Let's see if you held up to your end of the bargain."

"Trust me, Heaven, I would not lie to you nor lead you astray. I know what I'm doing." With that, they opened the over door and pulled out the angel food cake. It looked scrumptious. Parker saw Heaven observe the mold.

She tilted her head. "Remember that old saying... looks can be deceiving. We have to taste test it. This the moment of truth."

Parker turned the mold upside down, and the angel food cake fell exactly in the middle of the plate fully intact. No crumbs anywhere. Heaven looked on the countertop. She had left freshly cut strawberries to place on top, in addition to drizzling chocolate syrup down the sides. She would wait to place the whipped cream on top. Parker paid attention to detail as well. He grabbed the chocolate syrup and drizzled the strawberries.

Both stepped back to admire their finished product. "It's too pretty to eat," Heaven told him.

"No, it's not," Parker laughed. He sliced a piece for both of them. Heaven closed her eyes. It was delicious. It was the cream of tartar that had been missing. It did not overpower the cake, but enhanced it. Parker could not believe it. He had been taken back in time to the kitchen with his mother. This was really good. There was no pretending.

They each finished their slice and began the clean-up. Heaven told him she would put all the supplies and ingredients away, if he could wash the dirty dishes, since she knew where everything needed to be returned. Parker laughed. "Yeah, yeah, you just want to watch me wash dishes. I know how to do that, too."

Heaven wanted to comment she bet he knew how to do many things well, but she kept it to herself. She was playing with fire. Right now, she did not want to get burned. She was almost through, when she heard Parker comment, "Are you entering?"

Heaven's brow drew up. "Entering what?"

Parker pulled the flyer from the side of the industrial refrigerator where a magnet was holding it. "This contest. The baking contest."

"I don't know yet. It would be a dream to win. I would take the dollars and purchase a warehouse to store food for the shelter for the children and animals. I don't know that I'm good enough. My only specialty is what we just baked together – angel food cake. Plus, I don't have the entry fee. But if I decide to enter, I'll let you know."

Parker was reading the flyer for the rules and only half heard Heaven's reply. There was a children's division, a women's division, a men's division, and then a couple's division for the bake-off contest. He needed to review the rules more. "Do you mind if I take this with me?" he asked Heaven.

"No, feel free. I have another at my home."

CHAPTER 16

As they were locking up the bakery doors, Heaven did not know if her mind or her ears were playing tricks on her. She could have sworn she heard Parker make a statement that after reviewing the rules, he would get back with her to discuss.

Discuss what? What was there to discuss? If she would enter or not? No big deal. And was he going to enter as a contestant? A lot of questions going through Heaven's mind. This evening had not gone as planned— or did it?

Parker had walked to her car. He opened the door and made sure she was seat-belted in, and without warning, he leaned in and kissed Heaven and told her he would see her later. She watched as he got into his car and drove away. She could not start the car. He would see her later. When? Where? She could not think about this. She needed to get home and let Malcolm out. The evening had lasted longer than Heaven had anticipated. Malcolm was probably pacing the kitchen floor. She hoped TeeTee had remembered to place down the pee pads as a just-in-case precaution.

She pulled into the driveway. The front porch light was on. Heaven was thankful that TeeTee had followed her instructions to leave one nightlight on in the house. Malcolm did not like the dark. Heaven always left a nightlight on. She unlocked the front door, and immediately, the barking began.

"It's just me, ya big galoot." Heaven stepped over the baby gate and would have been knocked down if she had not prepared herself for the routine that always followed by Malcolm. She sat on the kitchen floor, and immediately, Malcolm began sniffing. The hair on his back raised, and he backed away. "Oh, stop. No one is going to take your place. You just smell his scent. That's it. Come here, Malcom." Malcolm did as she commanded. He nudged his head into her hands and then placed his paw on her leg. "I know, I know, you're ready for bed. So am I," Heaven kissed him on his cold, wet nose.

As she headed to the bathroom with Malcolm in tow, her thoughts went back to that one statement that Parker had made about the baking contest, "I'll get back with you." What did that mean?

Parker turned into his home. He could not go in just yet. Well, this evening had not gone as planned. There was no script. He had never turned down sex. What was wrong with him? He kept going over the evening's events. Why had he stopped? She was beautiful. When she looked into his eyes, time had stopped. It was just him and her, and yet, he could not. *Wait until Alex hears the story of this baker, Heaven, and of her delicacy of angel food cake,* he thought. He knew Alex would tease him relentlessly.

Parker got out of the car, unlocked his front door, and walked in. Silence. Darkness. For the first time, Parker noticed how lonely the inside of his home was. Of course, there was décor and furniture. There was everything here that Parker needed, except one thing was missing. He had not taken the time to contemplate this until tonight. Was it because she had left him wanting more?

Holding the flyer in his hand, Parker unrolled it. Competition was his middle name. Not many knew of Parker's baking skills. Tonight, he had shared a bit of his past with a stranger. He wanted to share more with her. As he read the flyer and the rules of the competition, he felt something foreign to him. Excitement. He knew they could do it. They could win, and she would have the dollars needed to purchase her dream – a warehouse.

It seemed pretty simple to him. The deadline was tomorrow. THE DEADLINE WAS TOMORROW! Had Heaven noticed the date? He would not be able to swing by the bakery until later tomorrow afternoon. It needed to be completed ASAP. He would complete it tonight and take it into work and then overnight it to have a record of it being mailed on time, along with a check.

Parker sat the kitchen table for what seemed an eternity. He knew it had only taken him about 30 minutes to complete the competition form. He wrote a check and placed it to the side of the table. *She's gonna be madder than a wet hen.* Parker smiled. He could only hope.

CHAPTER 17

Heaven pulled up to the bakery. TeeTee was unlocking the bakery. She heard the car door close and turned to see Heaven walked towards her. She kissed her on the forehead, as she had done since meeting Heaven, to greet her good morning. "Let's get inside and get set up. You promised our customers some fresh angel food cake samples. I sure hope it's good."

The morning had been busy. All the regulars, of course, had been coming in to get their usual, and there had been a few new ones. Heaven thought she would have no time to think of him. Wrong. Oh, so wrong. She had done nothing BUT think all day about him. She wondered if he was thinking about her and the events of the evening.

He arrived at work on a mission. He could not remember if he had even parked in his "normal" parking spot. He needed to make copies of the registration and then overnight it. He walked to his assistant's desk. Lanie had been with him going on five years. Lanie knew where Parker needed to be every minute, every hour of the day. He stopped at her desk and coughed.

Lanie had watched him walk to his office, pick up some documents, and then head her way. She knew that walk. He didn't know how to ask her how to do something personal. So, he would cough and then wait.

She laughed. Might as well put him out of his misery. "Parker, what do you need?"

How did she know? "Yes, I need your help in overnighting these documents. Before you call the service, can you make copies and place them on my desk? I need to meet with my father briefly."

Lanie nodded. "Yes, go on. Go meet with your father. I'll handle the rest from here."

Lanie watched as Parker walked down the office hallway headed towards his father's office. Something was up. Parker very rarely met with his father in the mornings. This must be important.

Parker stopped in front of his father's door. He needed to finish the conversation that had been started last night, before Parker entered the bakery. He knocked on the door and heard his father state, "Come in, please." There had never been a warm welcome to his father's voice. He was very straight and narrow. There was no gray in anything. It was either black or white, NO middle.

Parker walked in. "Good morning, father."

Parker's father turned around. "I have meetings

this morning. I will cut to the chase. The young woman you met at the shelter is nothing but trouble. I checked into her background. She appeared here in town a few years ago. There is no record of where she came from, and you know what that means?"

Parker did know what that meant. His father was stating in no uncertain terms to rid himself of any relations with this "young woman".

Parker looked at him. "Too late, we have entered a baking contest together." Parker knew that would catch him off guard. And it did. The expression Parker knew all too well. It was not one of disappointment, but one of displeasure. Ever since Parker's mother had passed, his father had worked long hours at the office. Parker rarely saw his father outside of the office. He looked at his father. He could not remember the last time he had seen him smile or even heard his father's laughter.

"You have no idea what you are talking about. She is not trouble. I spent the night with her..." began Parker.

Before he could finish the sentence, his father raised his voice "I'm sorry, you did what with her?"

Parker smiled. "Not in the way, you're thinking. We spent time baking. I shared mom's angel food cake recipe."

"Why?" his father asked.

Parker looked at his father. "She needed my help. I offered. Plain and simple."

"No matter what has taken place, I am advising against you seeing this young woman. We have no knowledge of who she was before she came to this city. The company cannot take the risk, nor be susceptible to bad publicity."

Parker turned away from his father. "Always about the company, never about the employee. I'll be baking with her. You are more than welcome to attend the competition or not. It makes no difference to me."

His father shook his head. "Mark my words, you will regret ever meeting this girl. I know her type. She will not stay here long. Do not set your sights on someone who will flee when the truth is revealed."

Parker nodded. It was best to leave before something hurtful was said. He could tell by his father's furrowed eyebrows, there was no changing his father's mind. Let alone convincing his father that Heaven was not who he thought she was.

Parker walked back to his office. He began to look at the client file that would need his attention. He stared at the file for quite some time and then decided to open it and review the documents inside. Thirty minutes passed. Parker was not in the mood. He could not concentrate. His mind was thinking back to last night and to her. He did not hear the knock at his office door. He did not hear his door open. He did not even realize that Alex was standing there until he heard the clearing of his throat.

CHAPTER 18

"A penny for your thoughts. Better yet, I know what they are. It's her," Alex told him.

He looked up. "I baked with her last night," Parker stated.

Alex laughed. "Is that what they are calling it now? Baking? My curiosity is piqued. Pray tell, what did you bake?"

Alex could not help but smile. This was not like Parker. He was a man in control, especially with his feelings. His best friend was smitten. He knew it. Parker just didn't realize it. He could not wait to hear about the rest of the evening.

Parker told him only bits and pieces of the evening and ended the story with the fact that Parker still had baking skills. Alex nodded and smiled, "Whatever you say, Parker. I'm sure nothing took place that you could not handle. Let's go grab lunch. Better yet, let's go grab dessert." Parker agreed. He was hungry.

Walking outside, Parker tilted his head. "I'll drive. I want to show you something." Alex knew where they were going. They were going to see her. Parker wanted to surprise Heaven. He needed to see her. The feelings of protection were resurfacing. He could not put his finger on it, but Parker knew his life would never be the same.

Pulling into the bakery parking lot, Parker was surprised at the business. The Achy Bakery Heart was packed. Alex chuckled. "It's popular today. Wonder what's baking."

"Funny, you're such a comedian. Come on," Parker told his best friend.

Parker could see her from the outside window of the bakery. She was laughing with several of the patrons. She came from behind the counter and hugged the two patrons she had been talking to. Parker needed to be that patron. What a way to start a day. A hug. Just a hug. Parker's mother made a habit of hugging him. For big reasons, for small reasons. She told Parker everyone needs a hug. Plus, hugs make you feel better. He could not argue with his mother. A hug always made him feel better.

Parker felt Alex nudge him in the side. "Okay, lover boy, are we going in, or are you just going to stare at her and make it even more creepy? Hopefully, after you baked together last night, she won't think you're stalking her."

Parker sighed. Leave it to Alex to bring him back to reality. "Come on. I want to tell her what I did." As they entered, the bell rang to make all aware another customer had entered. Those inside turn around to see who it was. TeeTee and Heaven glanced, as well.

It could not be. That was not him standing there in the bakery. TeeTee whispered so only Heaven could here. "Well, well, I would say last night was a success. Let's see what he likes." TeeTee placed her hand on Heaven's back to push her forward. Her feet were frozen. Heaven was grateful for that little nudge. She walked towards Parker and his friend. Heaven remembered he had volunteered with Parker that night at the shelter.

She walked towards them. She was watching for any reaction from Parker. Any change in his face. Parker began walking towards her. He came close to Heaven and before she knew it, he had reached for her hands and pulled her close to kiss her on her forehead.

"Good afternoon, Heaven. Did you get some rest last night? Dream of anything or anyone in particular?" Parker questioned her. She could not believe he had just kissed her and in front of GOD and everyone at the bakery. All eyes were watching. No one was ordering. Even TeeTee had put down the trays to observe.

"I did. I slept like a rock. Dreams, nah, not of anyone but of the competition. I need to complete the entry registration. Other than that, nothing significant." Heaven stated with little emotion.

Parker leaned forward. "Nothing significant? Okay, we'll play it your way. I do need to let you know that the deadline for that 'thing' we spoke about last night was today. Did you complete the 'thing'?"

Heaven squealed, "Fudge nuggets. I did not. I won't have the dollars until this Friday." Heaven looked at Parker. "I forgot. Oh my gosh. It totally slipped my mind. What am I going to do? I missed the deadline."

A tear trickled down Heaven's cheek. Parker reached with this thumb and gently wiped it away. "Heaven, I sent the paperwork and the fees in this morning. Overnight. It will be received on time. I took care of it." Heaven didn't know whether to be thankful or to be incensed that he did it without asking her. She took the thankful approach. "Thank you, Parker."

Without giving thought to his consequences, he leaned in and kissed Heaven on her lips. Let everyone watch. It was not a kiss of request, but a kiss of kindness. "It's no big deal. We have one week to prepare. Last night was just a stepping stone to see if we 'jelled' together. We did. We can do this." The only words resonating in Heaven's head were "we". Parker kept saying "we". He was going to do this with her. Before she could comment further, applause broke out in the bakery.

Heaven turned towards TeeTee. Her face was blood red. Not because of the news, but because of that kiss. Parker cleared his throat. "Can we get some goodies to take back to the office with us? I'll swing by after work, and we can discuss the competition." Heaven nodded her head in agreement. Words would not come out of her mouth. Alex had already paid and was waiting at the exit. "Come on Romeo. Juliet needs to get back to work. You've already got the town folk talking."

Parker took a glance back. She was watching him. *Sweet niblets*, Heaven thought to herself. He caught her in the act. Could she have been more obvious? She did not think he saw her. There was no way on this earth she was going to be able to bake with him, let alone be near him in such close quarters as the baking competition would require. What had she gotten herself into?

CHAPTER 19

The day had finally arrived. This was competition day. They had been mixing and practicing the etiquette of how to bake the best angel food cake ever. Two weeks of being in close proximity to Parker had just about shot Heaven's nerves. This day would determine her future. This day, all the pieces of the puzzle would fit. This was Heaven's dream. She needed to win this competition. This would allow Heaven to purchase the small warehouse at the end of town. This property would give Heaven the space needed to store all the donations of food and canned goods, in order to help the school children and the homeless shelter.

Parker had told her he would pick her up at 5 a.m. sharp and they would head to the competition together. She did not like to admit it, but she felt better knowing they would walk into the competition together. She would not be alone.

TeeTee had told all the customers the week preceding the competition that the bakery would be closed, so that all could attend and support Heaven and Parker.

Heaven stood in the bathroom looking in the mirror. This was not the same person who had run away with nothing more than her belongings in a garbage bag. She was a survivor. She was a doer. Her word was everything. If she said she would do it, she would. She took a deep breath. She closed her eyes. "I know you're there. I know you have placed a hedge of protection around me. I know the plans have been put into place. Thank you, Lord, for never giving upon me." She stepped back. This day was for Malcolm, Tee, the kids, and the shelter.

Malcolm heard the footsteps on the porch. And then the knock at the door. Malcom began to whine. He was on time. Heaven thought to herself. During the preparation / practice weeks, he had never been late. He was always down to the business at hand – tweaking the angel food cake recipe to make it the best it could be.

One last look in the mirror. Hopefully, she looked professional enough. She and Malcolm opened the door. He was standing in black pants, a white collarless, long sleeve shirt and black work shoes. He was not just handsome, he was sexy.

Parker had closed million-dollar deals. He played golf with several of the presidents from the corporations in town. He had spoken in front of thousands of people about the start-up of businesses. Today, of all days, he was nervous. Why? This was, more or less, a baking contest. Just a baking contest. As he stood on the porch looking at Heaven and Malcolm, he realized it was not just a baking contest; this was something extraordinary. He was baking for her dream. He did not know how or why, but Heaven deserved the very best. And he wanted to be the one to give it to her.

CHAPTER 20

"Good morning, Heaven. Good morning, Malcolm? Are you ready to tackle the world?"

Heaven smiled. "Is there any other way than to hit it head on?"

Parker grinned. "No. It's best to dive right in and do it. Let the angel food cake fall where it may."

She could not help but shake her head. "I thought it was 'chips' fall where they may, but so long as the judges like our angel food cake, it can crumble everywhere." Heaven watched as Parker automatically leaned down to pet Malcolm. Malcolm tilted his head, so Parker would have better access to scratch his ear. Heaven could not help but smile. That small gesture of kindness made the biggest impact with Heaven. TeeTee had told Heaven since their first meeting – you can always tell a person's true heart by the way they treat animals. If this were any sign, Parker had passed with flying colors. She knelt down to kiss Malcolm goodbye, as she had done since he rescued her. She whispered in his ear that she loved him. Malcolm licked her nose, and Heaven walked him to the kitchen and shut the baby gate.

As Heaven stood in front of Parker for a last-minute check, Parker placed his finger under her chin to pull her close. "That's what I like to hear. Conviction." He gave her a light kiss, unable to resist the innocence he saw in her eyes. It was a soft kiss, not too demanding, more inquisitive to see her reaction. If they did not leave this minute, they would not be competing. Parker stepped back. "Let's get Malcolm taken care of. Come on, Miss Heaven, before we are late. Malcolm, hold the fort down. We shall return victorious!"

She did not resist the kiss. She could not. When Parker's warm lips met hers, she responded passionately. It was only when she could not breathe for fear of fainting, she heard the word "late". They would be late for what? Heaven shook her head. She was in a fog. Lawd, she need not be so close to him. Her emotions were heightened just with him standing on the front porch.

She nodded in agreement. "Let me put Malcolm in the kitchen and lock the baby gate. I'll grab my purse and lock the front door." Heaven took one last look at Malcolm, watching at the baby gate. "Everything is in your car, correct? If so, we are set and good to go."

Parker stated with confidence, "All is in the vehicle. We just need to walk in and register and begin the prep work. We've done this over and over for two weeks. It's just like riding a horse or a bike. You can fall off, but you will always remember how to ride or pedal. Trust me?" She leaned over the baby gate and kissed Malcolm on his nose. He licked Heaven, as if to reassure her that all would be okay.

Heaven could not fathom why, but she did trust him. She trusted Parker. She looked at Parker and said with confidence, "I do trust you."

The ride to the competition was but an hour's drive. Parker and Heaven wanted to arrive early enough to plan the set-up. As Parker shifted the car into park, he turned to look at Heaven. He reached for her hand. He squeezed it gently to capture her attention. "We've got this, Heaven. We know what we're doing."

Heaven squeezed his hand. "I know. Have we done everything that we can do? There's just so much riding on this. We have to be perfect. It has to be perfect."

Parker grinned. "Come on, before you talk me out of this and yourself, too." Without thinking twice, he leaned over and kissed her. He suckled on her bottom lip. He pulled away and could tell he had the effect he wanted. "There, now you can think about that kiss and not the competition."

Heaven rolled her eyes and shook her head. Of course, he would add one more thing to her list. She did not want to give him the satisfaction of knowing, but he was already on the list before the kiss.

Walking into the competition, Heaven whispered, "Wow, there's a lot here, Parker. More than I anticipated."

Parker stopped and quietly stated, "Makes us stay sharp."

They both approached the registration table. The volunteer found their name, gave them their apron number, and directed them to their station. Walking in, Heaven did not know if she would recognize any of the bakers or not. She bumped into Parker. He had stopped dead in his tracks. "Parker? Parker? What's wrong?" He did not turn. "My father is here, Heaven. He's over to your right. I have no idea why he is here, but I am going to find out. I'll be right back."

Heaven could only watch Parker leave. She headed to their station to get the supplies and ingredients set out. There was no time to waste. She hoped and prayed that everything was alright between Parker and his father.

Parker did not have the words to say. Why was he here? What did he hope to accomplish with his presence? As Parker drew closer, his father walked towards him and guided him to a corner, where they could talk privately. "Before you start with the questions, I am here to support you and the young lady. I've seen the commitment you have put into this competition.

I know you will be using your mother's recipe. I just wanted you to know I'm proud of you."

Parker was dumbfounded. He was ready to tear into his father. Parker did not want to hear anything said against Heaven. He and Heaven needed to stay focused. His father standing in front of him was not in the game plan, nor in the day's itinerary. He looked earnestly at his father. His father was aging. Parker knew this. This moment, though, he realized it. His father would not be around forever.

He reached his hand out to his father. "Dad, thank you."

His father nodded his head. "She's waiting. She's been holding her breath since you walked over here. You may want to get over to your baking station before she passes out." Parker laughed. He knew Heaven had been watching the entire exchange.

CHAPTER 21

Parker had to. Whether it was to calm his nerves or hers, but he had to. When she was within reaching distance, Parker picked Heaven up and swung her around. She placed her hands on his shoulder. "Parker Stevens, put me down. Have you lost your mind? People are watching."

Parker could not help but smile as he slid her body down his. "Heaven, this day could not get any better."

Heaven placed her hands on his chest. "Yes, it could. With a win. I need you, Parker. Please don't ever leave me."

Well, if the pressure were not on before, it was now. He stood looking at her. He was not going anywhere. He would never leave her. He could not tell her this. The bake-off would be begin in ten minutes. The emcee made the announcement to stand behind their stations. Bake time was 35 minutes – wait time (or cooling down) was two hours.

Time was up. All one hundred entrants had placed their angel food cake entries on top of their stations.

The judges began the walk. Heaven and Parker stood at the corner of their station. There was nothing else to be done. There were three judges. Each took a sample from the entrants. Heaven needed reassurance. She reached for Parker's hand. He wrapped his pinkie around hers and winked at Heaven.

The entrants watched with anticipation as the judges made their way to the front. The top ten would be announced. And then, those top ten named would be called to the front one by one. Heaven could not breathe. She felt herself get lightheaded. Parker noticed. He pulled her in front of him and wrapped his arms around her waist. The head judge began the announcement of the top ten.

They had made the top ten. *What in the world? How in the world? This must be a dream.* It dawned on Heaven that they would need to take samples to the three judges at the front table. She and Parker would be asked what they had done to make their angel food cake extra special. She was not going to be able to talk. Parker would have to speak for them. She was too nervous. As their number was called, Heaven picked their plate up. The angel food cake had been decorated in chocolate icing, with white powdered sugar sprinkled across the top. Strawberries and blueberries had been placed with whipped cream to accentuate the colors on top of the angel food cake. Heaven watched as the judges tasted again. She could not tell whether they liked it or not. These judges were good at keeping stone cold faces.

Walking back to their station, Heaven did not feel good about making the top five. She stopped and turned to Parker. "If I haven't already, I want to say thank you. Thank you for being a part of this, but more thank you for understanding my passion."

With no intent other than to alleviate her anxiety, Parker kissed her. Heaven placed her head on his chest. "Parker, I don't know that I can stand this much longer."

"Just a few more minutes," he promised. "Here they go, Heaven, the top five. We got this!"

Heaven could not believe her ears. Parker Stevens and Heaven Raye had been called in the top five of over 100 entrants. Heaven looked at TeeTee. She had seen her walk in. Heaven looked to her for reassurance. TeeTee was giving her the thumbs up. Heaven mouthed "easy for you to say." TeeTee grinned and nodded. Without realizing what he was doing, Parker had done the same. He scanned the room to find where his father had been seated. He nodded in his head in approval.

And then it hit Heaven – what if they won? What if they actually won the competition? She never imagined she would be in the competition, let alone in the top five. Parker and Heaven watched as the judges conferred and then broke away from each other. They handed the emcee the paper, which held the winner of the competition.

The top five were called to the front. One by one, they lined up across the stage in front of the audience. As the runner-ups were called, they were given a plaque with their placement and then, pictures were taken. They were then whisked off the stage. Heaven and Parker looked around. It had come down to Heaven and Parker and another couple. They had made it into the top two. Heaven closed her eyes. What are the odds that Heaven and Parker would win the competition? What would happen if they did the top prize? Both Heaven and Parker turned towards each other. Parker looked at Heaven. He reached for her hand. Parker smiled "No matter, the outcome, Heaven, you deserve the very best."

The emcee began: "Please welcome to the stage, your first-place winners..."

EPILOGUE

"Oh, my lord, it's crooked. Can you just shift it a bit to the left? Wait... a tad more to the right. Maybe if you touched the bottom left, it would center itself better."

Parker could not help but look down at Heaven, exasperated with her direction. "Heaven Raye, you have five seconds to make the right decision before I come down this ladder and leave it as is. It looks fine."

"I'm not scared of you, Parker Stevens," Heaven exclaimed. Parker came down the ladder. He pulled Heaven into his arms. He held her tightly, as if his life depended on it.

"Before you critique it, step back and just look at it. It's perfect." Heaven turned in his arms. "It is, and so are you. Thank you, Parker. Thank you for making my dream come true. Heaven's Angel Food has a home now."

"Look at me, Heaven. I did not do anything special."

Before he could finish his thought, Heaven interrupted. "Yes, you did. You believed in me."

Parker needed to tell her. He could not keep it a secret any longer. If a secret were told, then it was not considered a secret. This did not need to be kept a secret. He needed to share with her his feelings. She needed to know.

Parker took Heaven's hand and gently led the way inside to the warehouse. The warehouse Heaven had just purchased with the prize money. The warehouse that would house the food for the shelter and for the children of Windermere and so much more – oh the possibilities were endless.

"I love you, Heaven Raye. I have known this since we practiced those two weeks before the baking competition. Since you've been in my life, I smile a lot more than I used to. I'm jealous of your bakery customers who get to see you every day. I want that gift. I want days like those. I want to see you every day."

Heaven could not believe her ears. He was in love with her. She reached up to place her arms around his neck. She pulled him close to her. "I knew that day you walked into the bakery you would become a part of my life. God placed you in my life at just the right time. You rescued me."

Both Parker and Heaven watched as Malcolm closed in on them. Heaven could hear TeeTee in the back of the warehouse, urging Malcolm to go on. He stopped right in front of them and leaned his head in to Heaven's hand, approving what both Heaven and Parker knew.

Rescue and love go hand in hand OR is it paw?

SPECIAL DEDICATION

This book is based on a true story. The female character in this book made a difference in so many lives, and this is exactly what the beautiful young lady in real life has done. Heaven Nicole Redmon is establishing a non-profit charity called "Heaven's Angel Food".

I have been blessed to know her since she was seven years old. Not only does she have a heart for service, but her love for those less fortunate and walking the path she has taken, is shown daily by her actions of kindness.

She exemplifies God's word: Psalm104:28

"When you give it to them, they gather it up;

when you open your hand, they are filled with good things."

I know you will see what I have seen – a miracle. God's guiding hand leading her on a journey. A path designed only for her in HIS infinite wisdom. She has the most incredible family and a village that surrounds her daily with encouragement, support and most of all love.

For further information, please find Heaven on Facebook at Heaven's Angel Food.

KENTUCKY ROMANCE AUTHOR

The Day You Go from Romance Junkie to
 # 1 Best-Selling Kentucky Romance Author

de de began pursuing her dream of becoming a romance author at the age of 30. Born and raised on the farm in Rooster Run, Kentucky, de de was raised on the core values of the 3Cs (kindness, caring, and compassion). Throughout her young adulthood, de de volunteered in the community with her family, and specifically, her grandmother, Bea. Growing up in the country, romance novels were her escape to another world. de de knew that one day, her dream of writing a romance novel would come true. Fast forward to 2018, when de de picked the book back up that she had begun in her early 30s. As in life, circumstances and direction change the course, BUT never the ending goal. Learning the industry and working with her publisher, Beyond Global Publishing, God opened many doors and many connections, and de de has never looked back.

de de became a published Kentucky romance author in 2018. She is the #1 best-selling Kentucky romance author of the Two Degrees Series, which features her son, Bo, as the male model. Little did de de know that her child would become the next FabiBo.

de de is working on her new series – RESCUE ME (animals and love), which will debut in 2021. The story of rescue, the story of love, the story of FURever. The first book title is *FURternity Leave – When All You Need Is Hope.* The second one is debuting in October 2021 – *Heaven's Angel Food – When You Deserve the Very Best.*

de de has served as a board member of The Dream Factory of Louisville, KY, Opal's Dream Foundation, Spalding University – Athletic Board, as well as volunteered with other charitable entities. de de received the coveted 2018 Spirit of Louisville Foundation - WLKY Bell Award for her volunteerism within her community and now serves on the board as trustee.

de de is active within the pageant industry. She is the co-preliminary director of the Miss My Old Kentucky Home (a prelim to the state /national of the Miss America system). In addition, she is the co-director of the Miss Hillview, Miss Buttermilk, and Miss Bullitt Blast Festival prelims (Kentucky State Festival).

de de is employed as a medical malpractice paralegal with the elite law firm of Dolt, Thompson, Shepherd & Conway, PSC.

FAMILY (family always mean I love you) and this is true in de de's life. So many kind-hearted folk have traveled the journey. She has been married over 35 years to her best friend, Scott, from high school. She has two sons and two rescued fur babies.

de de encourages others to live by HIS word – Acts 20:35.

It was going to be one of those Monday mornings. As Logan was jogging into the hospital entrance, he could see several others were in his dilemma. Running a bit behind. It was Logan's first day of his new travel assignment. He did not want to be late. Logan knew the first impression was the lasting impression.

Winter knew she could not turn away. This was the man she was in love with. This was the man she wanted to spend the rest of her life with.

"Two Degrees Hotter brings to life not just the story of love but the struggle that can accompany the every day journey. When something is so precious, it is worth the effort. There is a point of the understanding that in our lives there is always a moment somewhere in time that a connection is or has been made. True love is a never ending connection.

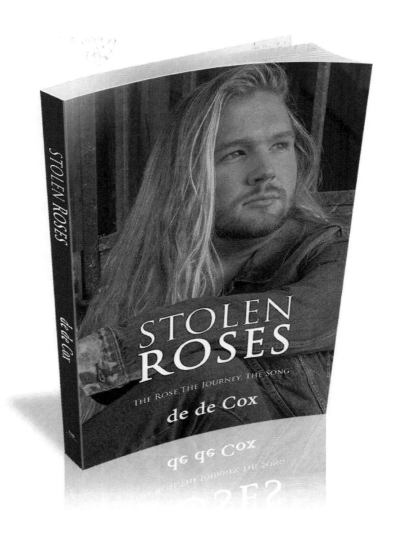

There could be no doubt. She read it multiple times. The note had said it all and yet, it said nothing. Never did she think that her heart could feel pain such as this. Plans had been made. He was her rock. He had been there since she was five. Growing up and sharing dreams, hopes, and goals had become their special time together.

The story of rescue...
the story of love...
the story of
FURever

ALL HIS LOVE FOR

Christmas

de de Cox

She shook her head at them. They had stopped. They would not move. The whining and barking were incessant. What in the world was going on? Why was it taking so long? As she walked towards the three, an uneasy feeling came over her. She drew closer to the edge of the road. Dr. Harper True, knew something or someone was down below. She could only pray that whoever or whatever was alive. As she slid down the embankment, her worse fears were coming true. It was not something. It was someone.